Amazing Daddy

For my Amazing Daddy

ORCHARD BOOKS
First published in Great Britain in hardback in 2016 by The Watts Publishing Group
First published in paperback in 2016
1 3 5 7 9 10 8 6 4 2
Text and illustrations © Rachel Bright, 2016
The moral rights of the author have been asserted.

A CIP catalogue record for this book is available from the British Library.
HB ISBN 978 1 40833 167 5
PB ISBN 978 1 40833 168 2
Printed and bound in China

MIX
Paper from
responsible sources
FSC
www.fsc.org
FSC® C104740

Orchard Books
An imprint of Hachette Children's Group
Part of The Watts Publishing Group Limited
Carmelite House
50 Victoria Embankment
London EC4Y 0DZ
An Hachette UK Company
www.hachette.co.uk

www.hachettechildrens.co.uk

Amazing Daddy

Rachel Bright

ORCHARD

My daddy is a **hundred** things,
A hundred things and **more!**

He's all the things
that you would think

a BRILLIANT dad is for.

He's big and kind and hairy.
He smells of safe and warm.

6:00AM

I love him from his top to toe,
From dusk right through to dawn.

I love
his morning
grumpy face...

. . . and his happy smile.

I love it when we
stay in bed to
snuggle up a while.

And when we're making breakfast,
If Daddy is in charge,
Whatever we are having ...

When he has to go to work,
I miss him not at home.
So, just in case he's
missing me . . .

. . . I call him on the phone!

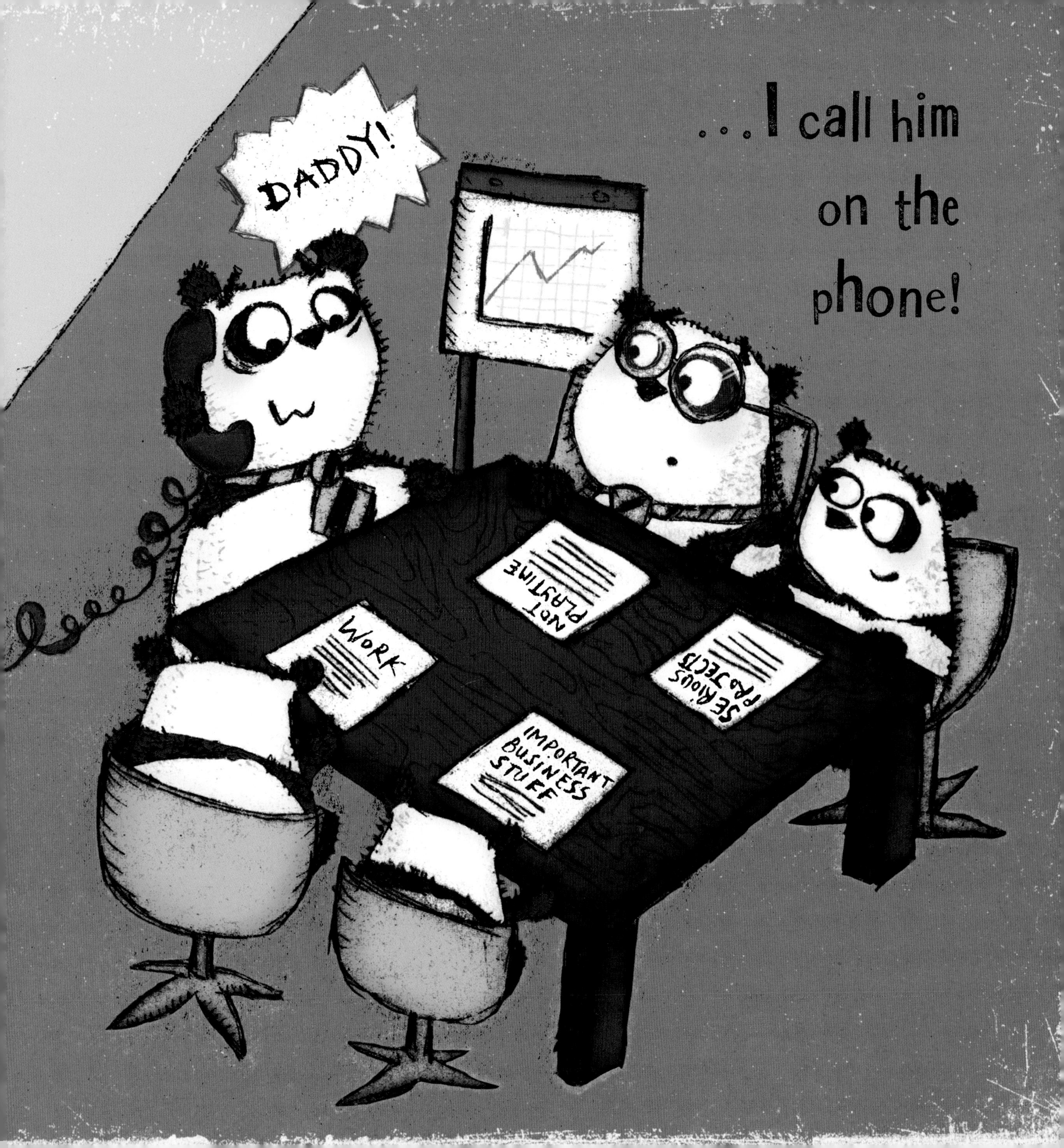

Often on the weekends,
he's busy in the shed.

He's got a lot of GOOD iDEAS
inside his daddy head!

And even when I'm naughty,
he doesn't get upset.

He just makes me think about it . . .

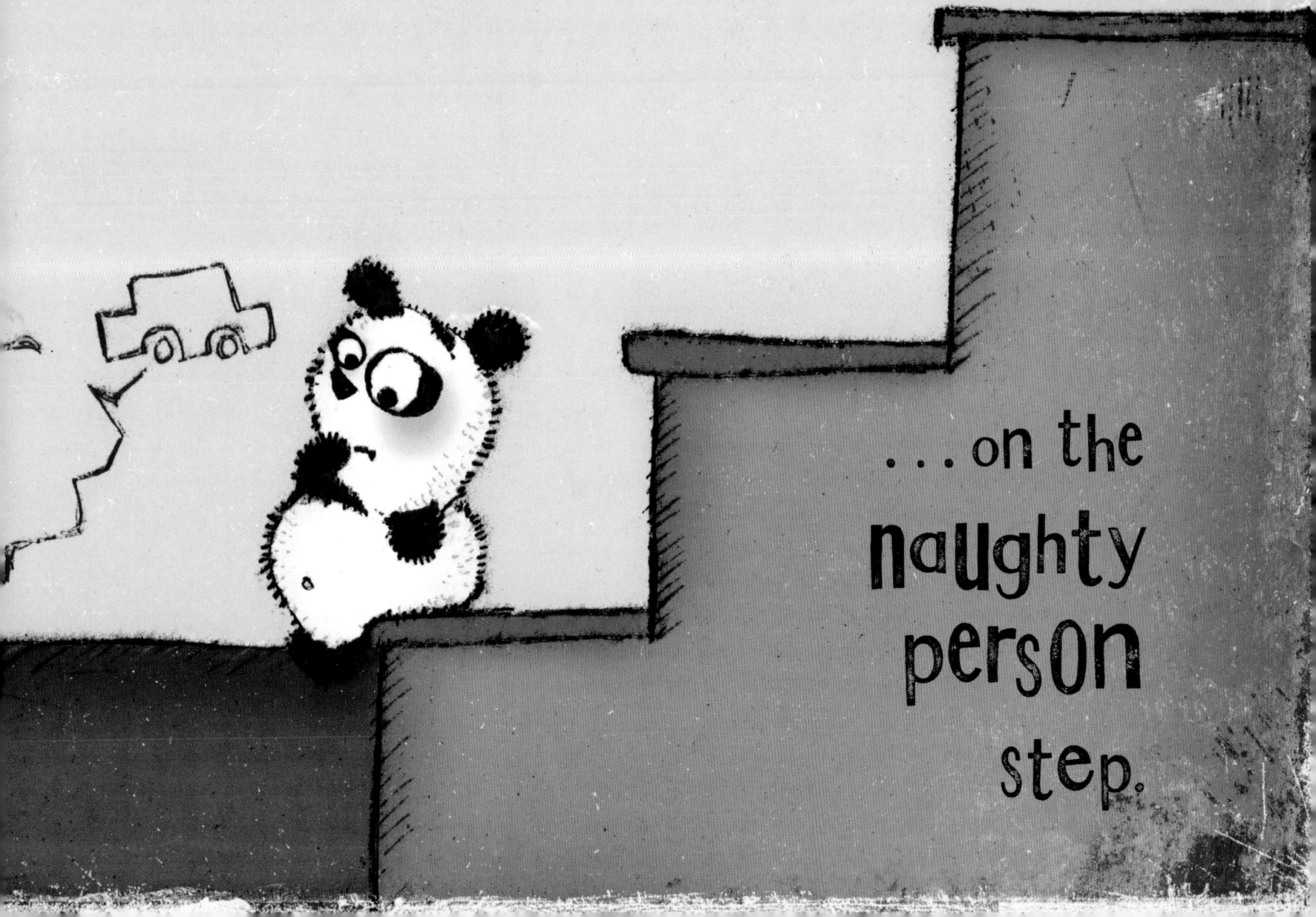

. . . on the **naughty** person step.

I love it when we
play all day
in scrambles, rolls and climbs.

And if I'm getting tired,
he will carry
me sometimes.

Yes, I'd like to be like Daddy
when I'm **big** and **old** one day.

But the oldness that my daddy has is **VERY** far away.

My **favourite** thing is bedtime,
when we **bundle** in a heap.

He'll tuck me in
and **read** to me . . .

...until I fall asleep.

Some nights, if I'm lucky,
he'll doze off in my chair,

And even though

he snores quite

LOUD

I'd rather he was there.

Yes, my daddy is AMAZING for a thousand different reasons.

He's a year-round SUPERHERO,

a daddy for all seasons!

But, Daddy, it's not Only

the hundred things you DO...

. . . that make you so AMAZING,

That make you just so
YOU!
It's all the days of you and me,
The Daddy times so far . . .

Daddy, this amaZingness, it's simply...

...who YOU are.